John Brougham

Playing with Fire

An original comedy, in five acts

John Brougham

Playing with Fire
An original comedy, in five acts

ISBN/EAN: 9783337102388

Printed in Europe, USA, Canada, Australia, Japan

Cover: Foto ©Andreas Hilbeck / pixelio.de

More available books at **www.hansebooks.com**

PLAYING WITH FIRE;

An Original Comedy,

IN FIVE ACTS,

BY

JOHN BROUGHAM,

AUTHOR OF THE FOLLOWING

PUBLISHED PLAYS:

The Demon Lover, The Irish Emigrant, Life in New York, A Decided Case, Temptation, Love and Murder, O'Flanagan, The Irish Yankee, The Red Mask, Columbus, Dred, All 's Fair in Love, Franklin, The Gunmaker of Moscow, The Game of Life, The Game of Love, Romance and Reality, Dombey and Son, David Copperfield, Jane Eyre, The Musard Ball, Tragic Revival, Neptune's Defeat, Shakspear's Dream, Dark Hour before Dawn, Art and Artifice, The Miller of New Jersey, Take Care of Little Charley, Pocahontas, Night and Morning, etc., etc., etc.

MANUSCRIPTS:

...s in the Web, The Mysteries of Audley Court, The Duke's Motto, Bel-emonio, Might of Right, or Soul of Honor, The Sculptor of Genoa, Death Fetch, Phantom Captain, Golden Dream, O'Donnell's Mission, etc., etc.

Note.

PLAYING WITH FIRE;

Originally played at WALLACK'S THEATRE, New York, October, 1860;
and first performed at the PRINCESS' THEATRE, (under the management of Mr. A. Harris,) on the 28th day of September, 1861.

Characters.

	Wallack's Theatre.	Princess' Theatre.
Herbert Waverly	Mr. W. H. Norton	Mr. G. Jordan.
Doctor Savage	Mr. J. Lester Wallack	Mr. John Brougham.
Uncle Timothy	Mr. W. R. Blake	Mr. Ryder.
Pinchbeck	Mr. A. H. Davenport	Mr. Widdicomb.
James	Mr. Oliver	Mr. Jones.
Mrs. Herbert Waverly	Mrs. Hoey	Miss R. Leclercq.
Mrs. Doctor Savage	Miss Mary Gannon	Miss C. Leclercq.
The Widow Crabsticke	Mrs. Vernon	Mrs. Weston.
Perkins	Miss Carman	Miss Honey.
Mary Anne	Mrs. Tree	Miss Price.

TIME—PRESENT.

Costumes—MODERN.

PERKINS must wear in the 4th and 5th Acts a similar dress to Mrs.
WAVERLY'S in the 1st.

PLAYING WITH FIRE.

ACT I.

SCENE.—*The Consulting Apartment at Dr. Savage's—doors*, L. C., R., *and* L.; *window*, R. C.; *table*, R.; *sofa*, L.

Enter PINCHBECK, C.

PINCHBECK. The Doctor not down yet. Now for my studies. A medical practitioner I am resolved to be, somehow or other, it only wants a tolerable share of impudence, and a few of the regular phrases; *half* the capital I know that I possess already—the other half I'm picking up daily. Ah, here are a couple of stray prescriptions to add to my stock. (*picks up prescriptions, and puts them in pocket-book*) I wonder how my other profession gets on. Let's see if there's any chance of a nibble this morning. Hallo! my advertisement not in?—yes, here it is. (*reads*) "Matrimonial.—A professional gentleman, of good social position, knowing how many people are deterred by an unconquerable timidity from avowing their preferences, and, instigated by a spirit of humanity, has established a secret agency, through which the happy union of congenial temperaments can be effected in the most confidential manner.—Apply, &c." My correspondence has not been voluminous as yet. Ah, here's another bite from a cautious kind of fish, who has been nibbling at the hook recently. (*reads*) "Romeo will be at W.'s office, to-morrow, at twelve." Hurrah! this looks like a capture, I think; the Doctor always makes his calls at that time, and the coast will be clear for my operations. Meanwhile, I must read up for my medical character. (*takes book and reads*) "Diagnosis of diphtheria: palate hard and dry, throat parched"—how very singular, I feel these symptoms every day, just about this time—"remedy:

a strong dilution"—nothing like prevention; I shall pre-
scribe for myself, at once—strong dilution; I don't know
anything stronger than brandy. (*goes to cupboard, and
mixes some brandy and water*)

Enter PERKINS, *door*, L. C.

PERKINS. My gracious, what are you doing Mr.
Pinchbeck?

PINCH. (R.) Picking up a little practical knowledge in
physics, my dear—manufacturing the brass for my professional door-plate by-and-bye. (*kisses her*)

PERK. (L.) You don't seem to lack the raw material,
Mr. Impudence.

PINCH. Fortunately, no—most essential ingredient in
the professional mixture; but how do we find ourselves
this morning—is our pulse regular, have we had a quiet
night?—let me see. (*feels her pulse*) Where the deuce is
it? Ah! I have it now—low, torpid, system wants
invigorating. Allow me—slight tonic. (*mixing glass of
brandy and water*)

PERK. (L.) I couldn't touch it for the world.

PINCH. Pooh, pooh—mustn't disobey your medical
attendant—case urgent—do you good—nauseous, I know,
but necessary.

PERK. (*drinks*) I never could—that's not so hard to
take—what a capital doctor you would make.

PINCH. I believe you—I've watched them closely,
dear—good deal of humbug among the medicals! Most
ailments you see are imaginary—we have to humour
those patients, study their characters, not their com-
plaints—that's the principle—tickle them up with cordials,
alcoholic balsams, and palatable medicated confections.

PERK. But if they should be really ill?

PINCH. Then we have nothing to do but consult, and
shift the responsibility.

PERK. Why, I declare you seem to be quite fit to go
into the doctory line yourself.

PINCH. I should think so, indeed. You don't suppose
that I have swept a doctor's office, and dusted his clothes
and books a whole year for nothing. Now, I have something else to say to you—I've got a wonderful nibble at

my matrimonial hook. You promised to assist me and go halves in the plunder, so you'll have to represent the eligible party to all the male gudgeons. I can manage the feminine department myself.

PERK. I'll do just what you say, for I do believe you are clever enough to make both our fortunes.

PINCH. That's right; now embrace me with respectful energy, and go attend to your business. (*they embrace*)

Enter DOCTOR SAVAGE, *door*, L. C.

DR. S. Hollo! what are you about there?

PERKINS *runs off.*

PINCH. Singular and sudden attack, sir—sort of what-you-call-em dance—beg your pardon for taking the liberty, sir—I was just looking at the book to see what it meant.

DR. S. I think *I* might see a walking volume of rascality without straining my eye-sight much, Master Pinchbeck; but you're a useful scamp enough, and so, until you make it too apparent, I suppose I must continue partially blind.

PINCH. Always glad of your good opinion, sir.

DR. S. That will do—be off.

PINCH. Real professional tone—I must practice that—be off! *Exit*, L. C.

DR. S. (*looks at slate*) No calls to make for an hour. I hope I shall be allowed to enjoy my newspaper; if there is one thing worries me more than another, it is to be interrupted in the middle of an interesting paragraph—anything new to-day. (*bell rings*) Now, isn't that provoking. Pinchbeck—Robert—not at home—not at home to anybody, mind!

Enter HERBERT, L.

HERB. All right, I'm *nobody*—door open; knew you wouldn't mind me—Julia's gone up stairs to your wife.

DR. S. My dear boy, of course, you are privileged always, but you must confess, that when a man who loves to devour his daily, is stopped at the very first mouthful——

HERB. Yes—I know—irritating, very—but it can't be helped now—no loss, however—I've read it all—nothing

in it—never is—stupid age we live in, my dear friend—
dull—money-grubbing, unromantic, unendurable! (*crosses*
R. *to* L.)

DR. S. Hollo! Herbert, how's this—touch of the
blues—eh?

HERB. Touch!—an avalanche—overwhelming, de-
structive !

DR. S. Indigestion.

HERB. Pshaw—feel my pulse.

DR. S.—Regular as clock-work.

HERB. Indeed—anatomical mockery—sanguineous deception. Look in my eye.

DR. S. I do—clear, bright and placid as a summer
lake.

HERB. But with an under-current of despair.

DR. S. Good gracious! you alarm me. What's the
matter?

HERB. I don't know—that's the misery. I'm a physio-
logical cheat—an animated subterfuge. This calm and
passionless exterior covers a heart tortured by anxiety.
I'm a sort of Spartan boy, with a continually gnawing
fox—a modern Prometheus, with an insatiable vulture
still feeding here. (*goes to sofa,* L.)

DR. S. On *pate de fois gras*—your liver's out of order.

HERB. Don't laugh; (*rises*) there's a good fellow. I'm
serious—like Othello, perplexed in the extreme.

DR. S. Not from the same cause, I hope.

HERB. No, no—I almost wish it were.

DR. S. The deuce, you do. Pray, explain yourself.

HERB. I will, if I can. Hark! isn't that Julia's
voice?—no. I wouldn't have her hear me for worlds.

DR. S. A secret, eh?

HERB. Yes—a most embarassing one.

DR. S. Aha, I understand.

HERB. No, you don't.

DR. S. Yes, I do. You married young.

HERB. Well?

DR. S. Nearly six years ago.

HERB. Well?

DR. S. And you have seen some one——

HERB. Stop! I won't allow your tongue to utter such

a sacrilegious thought. You know nothing about it. I love my wife more truly, more devotedly than ever.

DR. S. Oh, then, perhaps she——

HERB. No; I tell you—no—that's not it at all.

DR. S. Well, what is it, for mercy's sake—is she in bad health?

HERB. On the contrary, fresh and fair and beautiful as Hebe.

DR. S. And her spirits?

HERB. (L.) Ah!

DR. S. (R.) Now we're coming at it.

HERB. Are we! perhaps. William, I think I can count upon your friendship. (*goes up, and brings down chair and sits*)

DR. S. In any extremity.

HERB. Then listen to me, and let me have your advice. My wife is the victim of some concealed sorrow, the cause of which I can't divine. Since our marriage we have lived only for each other, as you know; the years flew by in calm tranquillity, happy in our mutual confidence, happy in our entwined affection.

DR. S. But surely——

HERB. Wait; not long since, only a few months ago, it smote upon my heart like a sudden stab that there was a something, I knew not what, wanting in our perfect understanding of each other. I could accuse myself of no concealment except of that one shadow of surmise; hour by hour, however, my suspicions grew to certainty; I could perceive that her gaiety was unreal, assumed, constrained, put on while we were together, only to be abandoned when she was alone. Well, one day I had just quitted her, and urged almost to desperation by the cruel doubts that oppressed me, I—I listened at her door, I—I looked through her keyhole, I did, William, I did; the hot blood sears my cheek for it, now, but I *was* that abject, cowardly thing, that miserably mean eavesdropper. Once, only *once*, upon my honour—honour?—*my* honour? Well, I was punished for it, amply, deservedly, when I saw the lie pass from her brow, and the truth, the terrible truth reveal itself: she *had* deceived me, the echo of the merry laugh with which she parted from me had scarcely died away, before I saw her gaze with a sad, painful expression upon the door I had passed through, and she wept—wept, I tell you, man, a flood of silent, agonizing tears, and I, who but a few moments before would have faced her lightest sorrow, at the peril of my life, my soul, felt a curse spring upward from my heart; but my great love compelled it back, and changed it to a grief. Oh, William, I could cry now like a child, like a child.

DR. S. And from as small a cause, no doubt.

HERB. You cannot question the sincerity of my suffering, or do *you* wish to deceive me also with a feigned indifference; in either case I———(*rising*)

DR. S. Stop; don't be hasty; I'm afraid you have been so already, conjuring up a spectre which may seem very hideous, and be nothing but vapour after all; let us look the phantom boldly in the face: how long is it since you made this grim discovery?

HERB. Three months and five days.

DR. S. There's nothing like being particular in dates, I presume you haven't hinted to your wife——

HERB. Of course not; do you think me insane?

DR. S. Not yet; nor given any indication by change of feature, or coolness of manner, that might suggest a suspicion to her.

HERB. No, at least, not designedly.

DR. S. But by accident? they breathe hard who wear masks always.

HERB. I can't tell, I believe not.

DR. S. At all events, she still plays the same part?

HERB. Yes, *plays* it, oh, how skilfully!

DR. S. You can't think of any reason springing from yourself—any slight jealousy or misconception?

HERB. None whatever.

DR. S. It's reasonable to conclude then, that the cause, whatever it be, must rest with her alone?

HERB. It must, it must!

DR. S. Bah, bah! hold your tongue, and above all, be reasonable; the cause of her uneasiness must be either real or imaginary—if imaginary, it must be dispersed for her sake—if real, it must be met manfully for your *own*. You've been a great deal in each other's society?

Herb. Necessarily—we wished for none other.

Dr. S. Perhaps not! Well, I confess I'm puzzled.

Herb. I made an excuse for calling that you might watch her closely without exciting her suspicion, there may be some lurking illness that your experienced eye would detect. (Mrs. Herbert *and* Mrs. Savage *laugh without*) Hark, she comes! (*crosses to* R., *behind table,* Mrs. Herbert *laughs outside*) Ah, that laugh—how it chills me—silence and discretion!

Dr. S. Pooh, I'm a physician!

Enter Mrs. Savage *and* Mrs. Herbert, L. 2. E.

Mrs. S. (*speaking as they enter,* L.) It's not true, my dear, for the newspapers say that the Empress wore them at the last ball, and I suppose that settles the question.

Mrs. H. (*joyously,* L. C.) Good morning, my dear Doctor, I hope you'll pardon me for not paying my respects sooner, but when women meet you know they have a thousand things to talk about.

Dr. S. (R. C.) Don't mention it, my dear madam, I'm delighted to see you looking so well.

Herb. Pale, isn't she?

Dr. S. No.

Mrs. H. (*to* Herbert) Did I detain you love?

Herb. (R., *gaily*) Not at all, darling—had a glorious chat with my old friend William—isn't that flush hectic?

Dr. S. Hectic? nonsense!

Mrs. H. (*to* Mrs. Savage) Don't you see a sad expression in his eye.

Mrs. S. (L.) Not a bit; I suppose I must introduce myself. (*crosses to him*) I believe I have the honour of addressing the celebrated Dr. Savage?

Dr. S. Eh, who's that?

Mrs. S. I'm your wife, if you please, Doctor.

Dr. S. Oh, little woman, is that you?

Mrs. S. Yes it is—and you take no more notice of me than if I were any other article of household furniture.

Dr. S. Ah, you little humbug, you want to give your friends an idea that you are terribly neglected, don't you?

Mrs. S. Well, and am I not, when I've hardly seen you for a week.

HERB.   { What?
MRS. H. { Is it possible?

MRS. S. It's a melancholy fact; what with calls out, consultations—very convenient excuses, and that odious club, ah, how I'd like to strangle it. I haven't set eyes upon him only for a minute or two, for—for—oh, ever so long. *(retires up stage and sits on sofa)*

DR. S. But didn't I come at last to comfort you as the other tyrant said, you perverse little pet grumbling domestic dictator. (MRS. HERBERT *laughs, sitting on sofa*)

HERB. Ah, that perfidious laugh.

MRS. H. Very good, Doctor; did you hear that, Herbert dear?

HERB. Oh, yes, my love, capital! *(laughs and turns up stage)* The mask, the mask, how evident it is.

DR. S. I know better than to let you have too much of my company, my duck.

MRS. S. Indeed, sir, and why, may I ask?

DR. S. Precautionally, my darling; I'm out of spirits sometimes, and dullness is contagious.

MRS. S. I'm much obliged to you for your consideration.

DR. S. Oh, you're very welcome.

MRS. S. But I think it more professional than polite; don't you agree with me, Mr. Waverly?

HERB. Yes, perfectly—I beg your pardon, I didn't exactly catch the——

MRS. H. Why, Herbert, dear, you seem out of spirits yourself to-day.

HERB. Not at all, my darling, what could induce you to suppose so? *(to* DR. SAVAGE*)* She has been crying.

                    (MRS. HERBERT *turns to* MRS. SAVAGE)

DR. S. I wouldn't be surprised, women frequently cry about trifles—seldom about troubles.

MRS. S. (L.) It's very evident, my dear, that their high mightinesses our respective lords and masters, have not finished their confidential chat.

HERB. I assure you there's no particular conference, we have nothing to consult about, have we, William?

DR. S. Nothing but the state of the weather.

HERB. *You* don't imagine that I have, Julia?

MRS. H. *(laughing,* L. C.*)* Why *should* I, dear, to judge

by your merry laugh, you must be as free from care as
I am. *(goes, L.)*

Mrs. S. Come, love, I want to shew you my new aviary.
I'm sorry to say, my husband's abominable neglect re-
duces me to the old maidenish resource of pets, poodles,
and parrots—did you hear what I said, sir?

Dr. S. No.

Mrs. S. You're a bear, and I hate you!

Dr. S. Thank you, I'm very much obliged to you.

Mrs. H. Oh, don't say that, dear, even in jest.

Dr. S. You wouldn't have her say it in earnest, would
you?

Mrs. H. How amusing you are, doctor; won't you
wait a little longer, Herbert?

Herb. Certainly, my love, as long as you please, I'm
not in a hurry. *(crossing, L.)*

Mrs. H. *Au revoir,* then. (Mrs. Savage *hits the*
Doctor *sharply on the shoulder, and as she goes off, turns
round and makes faces at him)*   *Exeunt* Ladies, L. 2 E.

Herb. (L.) Well?

Dr. S. (L.) Well!

Herb. What do you think?

Dr. S. Think? you'll pardon the force of the expression, I think you're a pair of fools, not having taken the
wise precaution to economise your domestic felicity, the
natural consequence has been a surfeit.

Herb. What do you mean?

Dr. S. Simply that your sky of happiness has been a
little too serene—

" Shining on, shining on, by no shadow made tender,
Till love falls asleep in its sameness of splendour."

Herb. Are you in earnest?

Dr. S. Profoundly!

Herb. And the remedy?

Dr. S. Establish a shadow.

Herb. As if it had not been all cloud.

Dr. S. I grant you plenty of cloud, but no storm.

Herb. Storm.

Dr. S. Yes, storm, the air never gets clear without
one; there have been enough of passing vapours, now

we must let the thunders roll, the lightning play, the rains descend.

HERB. You surely wouldn't advise a quarrel?

DR. S. By no means.

HERB. What then? do for pity's sake let me understand you at once.

DR S. (R.) Desperate cases demand desperate remedies. We must stimulate the organic system, the action of the heart is sluggish. You have every confidence in your wife's affection?

HERB. Unbounded!

DR. S. Wouldn't be afraid to put it to any proof?

HERB. Certainly not!

DR. S. Then couldn't you get some good-looking friend in whose honour and discretion you have reliance, to pay her just sufficient attention to excite an interest?

HERB. (*very loudly*) What?

DR. S. An indignant one, of course, anything to put an end to this torpidity of soul.

HERB. (*walks about*) Phew! you may well say a desperate remedy—it has sent the blood galloping through my veins at a stinging pace. (*crosses to* R., *and back to* L.)

DR. S. Yes, I know, it will do you good, too—vitalize your inertness, and fill you with wholesome anxieties in spite of yourself; wake up your slumbering energies, and pepper your flavourless existence with a little appetizing excitement.

HERB. What folly! I dare not resort to such an unworthy experiment.

DR. S. Are you afraid?

HERB. No, a thousand times, no.

DR. S. Then where's the danger?

HERB. The idea is so singular, but if I were to consent to such an extraordinary proceeding, where am I to find the friend?

DR. S. Oh, plenty of them floating about, who have nothing else to do.

HERB. Unless you were to undertake it yourself.

DR. S. What are you talking about?—good gracious! think of me, a plain, unpretending, jog-trot sort of person

—why, I never made a complimentary speech to a woman in my life—I don't know how—it's preposterous.

Herb. You recommended it yourself.

Dr. S. Yes, but it's rather a novelty in medical practice to ask a doctor to swallow his own prescriptions.

Herb. Consider, that in you I have the completest trust—besides, you'll know exactly how far it will be prudent to go. Come, come, I shall consider it unfriendly if you refuse.

Dr. S. Truly, a ridiculous position I have placed myself in. I'll tell you what I'll do, I'll compromise the matter with you by trying to find out the cause of her disquiet, and if I find myself floating towards flirtation, why, I'll resign myself to the current.

Herb. That's my good, kind friend. (Ladies *laugh outside)* Here they come, now you can commence at once.

Dr. S. What, while you are present?

Herb. Pshaw, that's of no consequence.

Dr. S. Oh, I thought it was; well, but my wife will be here too.

Herb. Yes, that's awkward.

Dr. S. So I should think.

Herb. Never mind, I'll pay my regards to her while you——

Dr. S. No, you won't do anything of the kind.

Herb. What, William, are *you* afraid?

Dr. S. No, certainly not—confound it, I begin to feel as if I had walked open-eyed into a nice predicament.

Enter Mrs. Savage *and* Mrs. Herbert, *door* l.

Mrs. S. What's the matter, dear?

Dr. S. Oh, nothing—I'm afraid I've given the wrong prescription to a patient, that is all.

Mrs. H. No danger, sir, I hope? *(crosses to him)*

Dr. S. Not at all—that is, at present—upon my life, she's remarkably pretty, I never noticed it before; I don't think it would be very difficult to say a few tender words to her—hem, Mrs. Waverly! *(she turns suddenly)* Bless my soul, who would have thought she'd turn on a fellow like a drawing-room tigress—beg your pardon, but did you——

B

MRS. H. No, sir.

DR. S. I thought not—did you ever read this interesting work—I don't mean that—if you would only grant me a private interview.

MRS. H. Sir!

DR. S. No, not private—public, I mean—oh lord! I don't know what I mean; see what it is to be unused to a thing—that's as far as I can go at present.

Enter PINCHBECK, *with coat, door,* L. C.

PINCHBECK. Cab's at the door, sir.

DR. S. Oh, ah—yes, to be sure—dear me, I had almost forgotten my visits. (*going*)

MRS. S. You're not going out in that coat?

DR. S. Bless me, no—excuse me—a little absent this morning.

(PINCHBECK *puts coat on* DOCTOR—*business—all laugh—*DOCTOR *runs off—Drop quick*)

END OF ACT THE FIRST.

ACT II.

SCENE.—*Drawing Room at Waverley's.*

Enter MARY ANNE, *followed by* UNCLE TIMOTHY, C.

MARY. What name shall I say, sir?

UNCLE T. Oh, ah! yes—nobody—anybody. Just say he's wanted, that's all.

MARY. Hem! Gentleman from the rural districts.

Exit, R. 2 E.

UNCLE T. Now look at this house: who couldn't tell at a glance that the beautifying influence of a wife made this home a very nest of comfort and happiness? bless my soul what a deal of time I have wasted to be sure, and yet, how it's generally arrived at I haven't the remotest idea; phew, the very thought sets me in a flame! I'm on the road now, though; where's the paper? ah, here—here is the fiat of my fate, the first step towards connubiality made easy. "Romeo will be at Mr. W.'s office at twelve to-morrow." I'm Romeo, kindly assisted in the pursuit of some anonymous Juliet by this benevolent mouthpiece of the diffident. (*takes out letter and reads*) " Dr. Savage, No. 34——Eh, bless me, here's Herbert! (*thrusts letter into his pocket*)

Enter HERBERT, R. 2 E.

HERB. Why, Uncle Timothy, is it you?

UNCLE T. (L.) Yes, my boy, it's Uncle Timothy, come to town incog, like a Crown Prince. Glad to see you. How's Julia?

HERB. In excellent health, and charming as ever.

UNCLE T. O, you lucky, happy dog.

HERB. Yes, happy ; very, very happy. (*seriously*)

UNCLE T. Anybody can see that. Aha, it's the only true felicity, my boy. I envy you, Herbert, upon my life I do. What's the use of all the enjoyment the world can procure if you have to lock it up in your own chest? It won't keep sweet unless it can get air, unless you can give it to somebody to take care of it for you, and even then you must take it out occasionally, like very good clothes, for fear the moth should get into it; toss it to and fro, from one to the other—I don't mean ridiculously, like overgrown children with a toy that might be lost or broken in the operation, but like a delicate gem whose lustre should only be renewed by your own hands. Why you'll forget you ever possessed it if you stowed it away in a drawer. Herbert, will you answer me one question ingenuously?

HERB. Yes, uncle, if I can.

UNCLE T. Do you think—now promise me that you won't laugh—do you think I—look at me well—that I'm, hang it, I can't go on, that I'm—I'm too old to marry. Phew!

HERB. Certainly not, sir, if——

UNCLE T. Yes, yes, I know, if I could find anybody to marry me.

HERB. I was about to say, if your inclination led you in that direction.

UNCLE. It isn't likely I would, you know, unless it did.

HERB. May I ask you in return, sir, have you any such inclination?

UNCLE. Well, yes—no—I mean it depends a good deal on circumstances.

HERB. What circumstances?

UNCLE. Never you mind, sir!

HERB. The astonishment to me is, that you never thought of it before.

UNCLE. How do you know I never thought of it? I *have*, my boy, dozens of times. Whenever I saw a truly happy couple, I was instantly inoculated with the infection, and looked about me eagerly to find a desirable partner, but before I could call up courage enough to ask the definite question, some accidental scene of domestic disquiet would be sure to send me back into my shell like a frightened snail.

HERB. This visit of yours is somewhat unexpected, uncle.

UNCLE. Yes, my boy, I'll tell you how it happened— Sister Patience and I were invited to a wedding about a month ago, and the delight of the young people made me feel so like a malefactor that I resolved to put a speedy end to my bachelor days. Now, our village is not an extensive place for matrimonial operations, and Patience is as watchful as a lynx, so I had to try a desperate manœuvre, and—well, you'll see what, by-and-bye. (*about to take a letter out*)

HERB. Is Aunt Patience with you?

UNCLE. (*looking round*) Bless me, no; since she lost her husband, old Crabsticke, and came to live with me, I have received the full benefit of her domestic experience. She used to worry the poor old fellow to the verge of lunacy, and now can't get rid of the old habit, and certainly does contrive to keep me in a blessed state of tribulation. Think of that, my boy—to have all the aggravating irritabilities of a duplicated existence without any of its little comforts, isn't it too bad. Why, what's the matter with you, Herbert, you're looking pale?

HERB. With me?—nothing, sir; never felt better in all my life.

UNCLE. Anything amiss between you and Julia?

HERB. Certainly not, sir. How could you imagine such a thing?

UNCLE. I don't know—partly on my own account; for, if my present resolution *could* be shaken, that, I think, would demolish it effectually.

Enter MRS. HERBERT, L. 2 E.

HERB. *Apropos!* here she comes to answer for herself. (*aside*) This state of dissimulation and suspense is maddening.

MRS. H. (*on seeing* HERBERT, *changes her manner*) Herbert here still! Why, I thought you had gone out, dear.

HERB. No, my love; Uncle Timothy here, intercepted me.

MRS. H. My dear uncle, I'm glad to see you!

UNCLE. (*crosses to her*) As I am, my little darling pet, to see you, believe me. You don't know, my dear niece, what gratification it affords me to see a truly loving and devoted couple—it convinces me what a procrastinating old idiot I have been all my life. But I have made up my mind, at last—how—well—no, now that I look at you again—not well?—why, what's the matter with your eyes—so red and swollen? Julia, you've been crying.

MRS. H. No, no; hush!

UNCLE. But I say yes, yes, and I won't hush. (*looking at both*) Hem! (*crosses to* c.) Hang it, I mustn't be too precipitate. There's something wrong between you two.

MRS. H.   ⎰ My dear uncle, no, no.
HERB.   ⎱ Not at all; you're in error, sir.

UNCLE. Oh, you can't deceive me. I've watched other people's matrimonial barometers too closely not to know the difference between changeable and set fair.

HERB. What an idea, uncle. (*laughs*)

MRS. H. Singular mistake. (*laughs*)

UNCLE T. Yes, yes, I see, these are very contemptible imitations of hilarity. I know exactly the state of affairs: as usual, I have blundered in at the wrong time, and find Master Hymen without his holiday dress—wedlock in *dishabille*. I was very right in supposing it to be an extremely hazardous investment, and so I'll have nothing to do with it. (*sits*)

HERB. (*sits*) What, my dear uncle, would you rather live a clockwork life, using your heart's machinery for no better purpose than to tick off the passing hours. Give me the extremes of joy and grief instead: and I won't allow you to mock your kindly disposition so far as to speak harshly of a state whose very anxieties spring often from an excess of happiness.

UNCLE T. I think I could contrive to do without the surplus.

HERB. But, sir, imagine the ample store of pleasures lost by those who journey through the world in single selfishness.

UNCLE T. A man can't miss what he never had.

HERB. But men generally envy what they can't obtain; who wouldn't seize upon a treasure that lay within his reach?

UNCLE T. Nobody if he had a right to it, and was assured of its reality.

HERB. Which can only be determined by the test.

UNCLE T. And then if it should turn out counterfeit, it would be too late for anything but the pleasant consciousness of having cheated yourself—doomed, moreover to have the consequence of your rashness tied about your neck—a heap of spurious coin that you can neither change nor fling away.

HERB. Ah, believe me sir, the real prize, though rare, if once obtained, is worth the risk.

UNCLE T. (*coming to* HERBERT) Do you really think so, Herbert?

HERB. I am sure of it. (*goes up to chair,* R.)

UNCLE T. (*to* MRS. HERBERT, *who comes down,* L.) Come here, pet; look in my face—tell me honourably and truly—are you contented? Do you love Herbert as much as ever?

MRS. H. A thousand times better, sir, but words are poor interpreters—the deepest affection is ever the most silent.

UNCLE. I believe you, darling; there's truth, conviction in that open glance. (MRS. H. *turns and sits* L.—UNCLE *goes to* HERBERT, *who is seated in chair,* R.) I think I *must*, after all. (*to* HERBERT) Nephew, between ourselves now, is your love for your wife as strong as it used to be?

HERB. So strong, my dear uncle, that my life's structure is sustained by that alone.

UNCLE. He's in earnest—they're both in earnest. I'll do it—*my* life's structure must be sustained. I've flung away joy and comfort too long. Herbert, won't you lodge me for a day or two? I have some very important business to transact.

HERB. (*rings bell*) Certainly, my dear uncle, as long as you please.

MRS. H. Nothing could give us greater pleasure.

Enter MARY ANNE, R. 3 E.

HERB. Mary Anne, shew uncle into the best of the spare rooms.

UNCLE T. Thank you—thank you! Yes, I'm determined, nothing can change me now.   *Exit*, R. 3 E.

HERB. (*after a slight pause*—MRS. HERBERT *rises and comes down*, L.—HERBERT, R.) I wonder, love, what chimerical project our eccentric relative has now in view.

MRS. H. I can't imagine, dear. Surely he don't contemplate matrimony himself?

HERB. I'm almost inclined to think so. Ah! if I dared approach the subject of my painful thought. (*aside*)

MRS. H. If he would but confide in me. (*aside*)

HERB. I shall at least give her an opportunity for explanation. (*aside*) Julia, dear, come, it's a long time since we had one of our confidential gossips together. (*they sit on ottoman*, C.)

MRS. H. He is going to explain. (*aside*) Ah! yes, Herbert, dear, and I have missed them so much. (*they sit*—MRS. CRABSTICKE *heard outside*—*they start up*)

MRS. C. Don't tell me any such nonsense as that.

Enter MRS. CRABSTICKE, C., *with umbrella and reticule, and* SERVANT.

MRS. C. How d'ye do—how d'ye do? Didn't expect me, I suppose?—exactly—didn't expect to be here myself yesterday—Thank you, I *will* sit down. Don't let me put you out of the way. Young man, take care of that umbrella, it is a family relic. Well, my dears, here I am, dropped down promiscuous-like out of the clouds, as a body

might say.   Why? I'll tell you why—*he's* here, isn't he?
Yes, I thought so—knew he'd come first.   What a worrit
he is ! it's well he has me to look after him.   I mistrusted
he had something on his mind, and was resolved to find
it out; did I ? why of course I did.   And now I have
travelled all this way by myself to fulfil a painful but
imperative duty.   I won't even ask you to give me a room,
for I mustn't be seen, especially by him, the old simpleton.

HERB. What's the matter, aunt? what has he done?

MRS. C. Nothing *yet* I hope ; but he's about to commit
an act of stupidity which would qualify him for a lunatic
asylum ! What? I'll tell you what in a few words.   I
noticed latterly that he had established a correspondence
with some unknown parties in the City, here—suspected
mischief, and felt it was my duty to counteract it. Did I?
of course I did ! So I got the servant to give me his last
letter, here it is. (*reads*) " Dear Doctor, since you assure
me that many happy matches "—the old fool—" have
been arranged through your assistance,"—the lying knave
—" I am strongly tempted to see if fortune will be
equally kind to me."—stupid dotard—" If I can get
away, for I am watched by a remorseless old catamaran,"
—that's what he calls his own sister—" you shall know
of it by looking at to-morrow's paper,—signed, Romeo."
What do you think of that ? Romeo ! the dear fascinating
youth ! Oh, couldn't I box his ears for him ! and look at
the paper, here it is; (*takes paper from her pocket*)
making an appointment for twelve o'clock to-morrow ;
that's nice conduct, I think.

MRS. H. To whom is the letter addressed ?

HERB. (*taking letter*) No doubt to one of those miserable scamps who trade upon human credulity.   What!
do I see the name and address of one of our most intimate
friends, Dr. Savage? Oh, there must be some singular
mistake here.

MRS. C. (c.) Not at all; several letters have passed
between them.

MRS. H. It will be easy to ascertain by questioning the
Doctor.

HERB. (R.) Nonsense, my love, I wouldn't insult him
by mentioning such a thing.

Mrs. C. Wouldn't you ? well, I'm not so squeamish;
I shall, you may depend upon it, and pretty smartly, too.

Enter James, c.

James. Mr. Pinchbeck wishes to see you for a moment,
sir.

Herb. Show him in.   *Exit* James.

Enter Pinchbeck, c.

Pinch. I beg your pardon, sir, for intruding so abruptly,
but the Doctor would be glad to see you for a few
moments, if convenient.

Herb. Very well ; I'll go at once. *Au revoir*, my dear,
good-bye, aunt ; I hope you'll be successful in your delicate undertaking.   *Exit*, c.

Mrs. C. (R.) So you think, my dear, that this Dr.
Savage's, or Savage (Pinchbeck *about to go*, c., *stops on
hearing name of Savage*) is the agent I am in search of?

Mrs. H. I'm quite certain he is not.

Pinch. Hah, what's this? one of my pigeons, I do
believe! (*makes signs to* Mrs. Crabtree)

Mrs. Good gracious, what's the matter with you, sir?

Pinch. If you could manage to give me a private interview, I think you might hear of something to your
advantage.

Mrs. C. (*shewing letter*) Do you know this person?

Pinch. (*aside to her*) Well, rather!

Mrs. C. (*to* Mrs. Herbert) Will you do me the favour
my dear, to keep my brother from seeing me while I
reflect upon the course I had better pursue.

Mrs. H. Certainly, my dear aunt, I shall gladly assist
you in the endeavour to prevent him from taking so
foolish a step.   *Crosses, and exits*, R. 2 E.

Mrs. C. Now, sir!

Pinch. (R.) Oh, my dear madam—my excellent, good,
benevolent looking madam—I implore you to cast a
pitying eye upon one whom a desperate fate has plunged
into a position at once repugnant to his feelings, and
distasteful to his principles.

Mrs. C. What on earth do you mean, sir?

Pinch. Hush! keep my secret, and I shall crown your

expectations with delight and happiness, without even asking you for the entrance fee to place your name on my books.

MRS. C. What books?

PINCH. My repertory of marriageable parties. I know the delicate nature of your mission, my dear madam; confide fearlessly in my discretion, preserve my unhappy secret, and you may choose from a score of highly available candidates.

MRS. C. Are you mad, sir? what is the man talking about?

PINCH. Suffice it to say, madam, in me you behold the veritable Doctor Savage, Medical Practitioner, Matrimonial Agent, Leader of Blind Cupids, and Door Keeper to the Temple of Hymen.

MRS. C. Are you Dr. Savage?

PINCH. One of them. There's another, a near relative— he is rich and prosperous; I am poor and struggling—*he* has blundered into position, through mere luck, while I have to cut my way through the world with the double-edged sword of cunning and invention.

MRS. C. Then, sir, your reputable relative don't know the estimable vocation you follow?

PINCH. Doesn't dream of it—but, as I said before, keep my secret, and I'll undertake to arrange this matter to your entire satisfaction.

MRS. C. Then you understand what I am here for?

PINCH. Thoroughly—saw it at a glance—no explanation necessary—I'll manage it for you.

MRS. C. I'm sure you're very kind.

PINCH. Don't mention it, my dear madam; it's my duty, my business—indeed, in the present instance, my necessity; for, as I have frankly told you how I am situated, it leaves me entirely in your power.

MRS. C. Do you imagine then, sir, that, with your assistance, I shall be able to take him back with me into the country?

PINCH. Oh, you'd like to take him back with you?

MRS. C. Certainly.

PINCH. When do you travel?

MRS. C. As soon as I can—I have no time to lose.

PINCH. (*aside*) I should say not.   The notice is short, madam; but we must accelerate our faculties.   You'll give me till to-morrow, to arrange preliminaries.

MRS. C. What preliminaries? Is there any more to be done than to let us meet anywhere out of this—there's no ceremony requisite?

PINCH. No ceremony—not immediately, I grant; but, pray, recollect I can promise no more than to bring about an interview.   Now, if the other party—you'll excuse the insinuation—should be dissatisfied with your appearance?

MRS. C. He'll have to swallow his dissatisfaction as well as he can; let him but cast his eyes on me, you'll see how quickly he'll surrender.

PINCH. (*aside*) Egad, the old lady has no mean opinion of her personal attractions. Consider the affair concluded, madam.   Do me the favour to give me a call at my office to-morrow at eleven o'clock precisely; we, professional slaves, who have our time parcelled out into mathematical slices, are compelled to insist upon punctuality.

MRS. C. I shall be there, sir, depend upon it.

(*as they are bowing ceremoniously to each other*)

END OF ACT THE SECOND.

ACT III.

SCENE.—*Same as Act II.—Evening, lighted up, curtains closed.*

MRS. HERBERT WAVERLY *and* MRS. DOCTOR SAVAGE *discovered.* MRS. WAVERLY *as though just parting with* HERBERT.

MRS. H. Good-bye, dear. (*they advance and seat themselves*)

MRS. S. My dear Julia, what a darling good-tempered husband you are blessed with, always in such excellent spirits; how happy you must be.

MRS. H. (*sighing deeply*) Ah, Fanny!

MRS. S. My goodness, how you sigh — what's the matter?

MRS. H. Fanny, the truth is, I'm miserable.

MRS. S. Oh, my dear, so am I.

MRS. H. Is it possible!

MRS. S. How could it be otherwise; just imagine the life I lead; your husband has always a kind word and a sweet smile on his lips, but my brute hardly ever condescends to honour me with a grunt.

MRS. H. But he loves you, Fanny.

MRS. S. Well, I suppose he does, in his bearish way; but I'm sure your husband doats upon you.

MRS. H. What makes you so sure of that, Fanny?

MRS. S. Because everybody can see he does.

MRS. H. Everybody except me.

MRS. S. I'm afraid, my dear, that you are rather too exacting. Ah, you should have my savage to deal with!

MRS. H. He is in earnest, Fanny—honest and sincere —notwithstanding his roughness; but the respect and affection which you and everybody see exhibited towards me are nothing but pretence and mockery.

MRS. S. You surprise me indeed; why I looked upon you as perfect models of domestic felicity!

MRS. H. So we were until I made a fearful discovery. (*they sit down*)

MRS. S. You interest me, dear. What discovery?

MRS. H. That something or somebody had estranged him from me.

MRS. S. Ah! I see; there's a little jealousy in the matter.

MRS. H. Oh, no, no, it isn't that; my own self-respect prevents me from entertaining so vulgar a suspicion.

MRS. S. My gracious! what can it be else.

MRS. H. I know not. I can scarcely define my sensations. A thousand petty circumstances have accumulated by degrees, until the conviction forced itself upon my unwilling mind that there *was* a change, but from what cause it is impossible for me even to guess.

MRS S. Dear me, dear me. I didn't think there was anybody unhappy but myself—I'm so sorry. (*rise*)

MRS. H. It has somewhat relieved my overburthened heart to share its secrets with you, my kind friend—for I believe I can confide implicitly in you. Advise with me, dear Fanny, what am I to do; this uncertainty is more than I can bear, and to persist in such a life of mutual deception would be unworthy and humiliating.

Mrs. S. I don't know really how to counsel you; I never met with a case like yours, seeming to love each other so devotedly—and yet, by-the-bye, *do* you love him? Excuse the bluntness of the question.

Mrs. H. Do you love *your* husband?

Mrs. S. Oh, that's a different thing; we make no such pretence.   My insensible brute don't seem to care whether I love him or not, and so I never ask myself the question.

Mrs. H. Ah! if I could arrive at such indifference, but it is Herbert alone who is blest with so apathetic a temperament.

Mrs. S. I don't believe it.   The fact is, my dear, you haven't managed him properly, depend upon it; these men are strange, cross-grained institutions.   If one of the born tyrants is perfectly certain that a conquered heart is his alone to domineer domestically over, he's apt to become either cranky or careless.   Now, when my delectable lord and master inclines to either—which he does occasionally—I get up a little bit of a flirtation, and it's astonishing what a good effect it has.

Mrs. H. Fanny! why, I never dreamt of such a thing!

Mrs. S. Oh! I know it's very terrible and Frenchy, and all that sort of thing; but take my word for it, if you would only try it once—just in an innocent sort of way, you'd see how soon you'll bring his lordship to his senses.

Mrs. H. You're not—you can't be in earnest, Fanny. Why, the mere suggestion makes me tremble with shame.

Mrs. S. How nice, and good, and primitive you are, dear.   If there were any harm, do you suppose I would advise it?

Mrs. H. I hope not, Fanny.

Enter James, *with card,* c., *down* l.

Why, it's your husband, Fanny!   Shew him up.

Exit James, c.

Mrs. S. I have a capital idea; suppose you practise a little with my porcupine.   He doesn't know I'm here.

C

I'll give you leave. Ha, ha, ha! you won't find him very inflammable. I can listen to it all from the other room.

MRS. H. What folly! he's my husband's most intimate friend.

MRS. S. Of course he is; and must naturally feel an affectionate interest for his most intimate friend's wife. Here he comes. Let us retire and prepare for conquest! Won't it be fun?   *Exeunt,* L. 2 E.

Enter DOCTOR SAVAGE, C.

DR. S. Good morning—hem—not here! Well, so much the better. I'm not sorry; give me time for reflection. A pretty business I'm upon—truly, a very nice employment for a middle-aged married medical practitioner, commissioned to do the fascinating, with *malice prepense,* to serve a friend; I—who never could muster up many sweet sentences on my own account. Hang me if I know how to begin!—phew! I wish I hadn't undertaken it. I didn't arrive at the absolute extent of my impertinence until I came to put it in practice; it's not an easy thing to do when a man's heart, if he be possessed of that anatomical superfluity, is interested; but to administer a dose of admiration with professional *sàng froid* is something unparelled in practice. I'd better go back to Herbert—confess my cowardice, and—yet, no, I'll do a deed of heroism worthy of the classic age; I'll devote myself to ensure the happiness of my friend, by arousing her indignation I shall give her heart vitality.

Enter MRS. HERBERT WAVERLY *behind him—crosses to* R.

She'll denounce my villainy of course; and shelter herself behind the affection of her husband; all will be explained by-and-bye, and——

MRS. H. Good evening, Doctor.

DR. S. Now, isn't that provoking? Just as I had made up my mind, in she comes like a beautiful phantom, and frightens all my ideas out of my head.

MRS. S. (*at* L. *door, aside*) Don't be alarmed: I'll be near you.

Mrs. H. How remarkably well you are looking, Doctor!

Dr. S. Yes, I thank you—I mean, do you think so? Yes, in pretty good health and spirits. Hem! now for my nefarious purpose: how the deuce shall I begin? Ah! Mrs. Waverly.

Mrs. H. What a sweet expression you have in your eyes this evening, Doctor. (*looking towards* Mrs. Savage)

Mrs. S. (*aside*) Good; that style will do to begin with. Look at him blushing.

Dr. S. I don't think I exactly caught your words.

Mrs. H. I was admiring the sweet expression of your eyes.

Dr. S. Were you? Yes, you're very good. (*aside*) What does the woman mean?

Mrs. H. They're blue, are they not? I do so love blue eyes!

Dr. S. They're not blue, ma'am; they're gray—cat-gray.

Mrs. H. Yes, blue gray: softness and brilliancy combined.

Dr. S. Hem! you're pleased to be complimentary, madam—slightly at the expense of veracity, to be sure; but, never mind that—how does my nose strike you?

Mrs. H. It's a heroic nose!

Dr. S. Thank you. I see you're inclined to amuse yourself at my cost. This strange turn of conversation has so confused me that I scarcely know where I am, or what I'm about.

Mrs. H. (*suddenly*) Doctor?

Dr. S. Madam.

Mrs. H. Will you do me the favour to be seated?

Dr. S. Certainly, my dear madam. (*aside*) What is she going to do now? (*as he goes to chair*)

Mrs. H. (*to* Mrs. Savage) Is that right?

Mrs. S. Nothing can be better; don't spare him.

Mrs. H. (*they sit*) Ah! my dear doctor, I ask you to call up all your pity, all your charity, invoke all the generous sensibilities which should interpose between man's strength and woman's weakness.

Dr. S. With pleasure, madam. What on earth is she driving at?

MRS. H. (*sighing deeply*) Will you be kind enough to close the door?

DR. S. Yes, ma'am. (*aside*) There's a vague fear creeping over me of I don't know what. (*goes*)

MRS. H. Doctor, can you keep a secret?

DR. S. Why yes, madam, I think I can.

MRS. H. Ah! but you know not the humiliating avowal I have to make?

DR. S. No, madam, not yet, but I shall know it, I presume—some wondrously important trifle, I've no doubt; you women have an unhappy facility for inflating small troubles, especially if you don't happen to be afflicted with great ones.

MRS. H. (*rises*) And you men, doctor, have a much more unhappy facility for misconstruing anxieties you have neither the sense to understand nor the sensibility to appreciate. (MRS. SAVAGE *signals to be careful*)

DR. S. Extremely obliged to you, madam, for the insinuation.

MRS. H. Why should women be judged by the same standard as yourselves; the active work of life which would bring with it equal health of mind, you deny them participation in, be they capable or not, and when thought wearied for want of occupation, or filled with fears which are perhaps too flattering, their very apprehension is made the subject of a jest, treated as ill humour, or passed over with mortifying indifference. (*going round*)

DR. S. (*aside*) Hush! my dear friend—good gracious, that will never do.

MRS. H. (*aside*) I declare I quite forgot.

DR. S. A nice little storm I've raised here—she's in a delicious mood for my nefarious purpose. I think I'll postpone the villainous design until a more favourable opportunity. Good day, Mrs. Waverly! (*going*)

MRS. H. Doctor! pray sit down again!

DR. S. Certainly, madam—rather an intermittent kind of person.

MRS. H. Pardon my extravagance—I'm quite sure that the parrot cry indulged in against women by the thoughtless or the unworthy, finds no response within your noble heart.

Dr. S. My noble heart, ma'am, as you're pleased to call it, hasn't had time to give so important a matter due consideration ; all I have to say upon the subject at present is, that the lines of duty and usefulness appear to be sufficiently defined in both sexes, and I most energetically object to the individual of either, who departs in the remotest degree from the naturally prescribed boundary.

Mrs. S. Truth, wisdom and philosophy combined, who could fail to be convinced while listening to those silvery accents?

Dr. S. (*aside*) Silvery humbug! This woman is either laughing at me or fast verging towards lunacy.

Mrs. H. Ah! Doctor!

Dr. S. What's the matter now, ma'am ?

Mrs. H. (*romantically*) There's a shadow—a cold, dark, desolating shadow on the sunlight of my life.

Dr. S. Then I'd advise you not to walk on the shady side.

Mrs. H. But how am I to avoid my fate ?

Dr. S. Cross over to the other.

Mrs. H. Alas I cannot ! A dangerous but irresistible influence compels me to linger in the gloom.

Dr. S. Shake it off, ma'am—you can if you like.

Mrs. H. It is impossible! as well might you tell your fever-stricken patients to cast away the sickness that subdues them. Doctor, I just now asked you to call up all your pity and your sympathy, let me implore you to do so now; I am about to put your friendship—your generosity to the severest test—listen to me mercifully, but don't look at me while I speak. (*puts her hand to his cheek*)

Dr. S. Yes, ma'am. (*aside*) What's coming now I wonder.

Mrs. H. I know as well as you do, Doctor, the duties and proprieties which should distinguish either sex—that to men is given the power of revealing the dearest tenderest thoughts without reproach, which women should preserve unspoken—think then of my agony of soul—imagine the intensity of a reckless passion which enforces me to quench all thought—defy all consequences while I avow that——

DR. S. You've said enough, madam, I understand you but too well, and would spare you further confession. (*aside*) Phew! what a thunderbolt!

MRS. H. No, no; I must disburthen my over-loaded heart entirely.

DR. S. I'd rather you wouldn't. (*aside*) Oh, my poor friend!

MRS. H. But I insist—it will relieve me.

DR. S. (*seating himself*) Well, if it will relieve you, go on, madam.

MRS. H. Shall I—must I tell *you* to whom my heart has fallen a willing victim?

DR. S. I don't want to know who the scoundrel is.

MRS. H. Ah, it's no fault of his—he's ignorant of the matter altogether.

DR. S. Indeed, then there may be time to avert a terrible calamity. Who is the villain—I mean the person —the——

MRS. H. Can't you guess—ah, Doctor. (*tenderly—falling in his arms—he throws her off—starting up*)

DR. S. Good heavens, madam, you don't—you can't mean me? (MRS. HERBERT *weeps*—DOCTOR SAVAGE *rises suddenly*)

MRS. S. (*aside*) Beautiful, my dear; couldn't be nicer— oh, what fun. (*at door*, L. 2 E.)

DR. S. You'll excuse me, madam—I'm not of the most diffident disposition in the world; but, really, the suddenness of this announcement has plunged me into a state of feverish embarassment. I didn't imagine—I wasn't aware—I hadn't the remotest idea that I possessed a single element of attraction—it's a—in fact—an emergency I never thought of providing against. Who could have dreamt of such a state of affairs. (*aside*) Stay—isn't it better to—the remedy is in my own hands. For my friend's sake, I must suppress the horror that her perfidy inspires me with, and, by continuing my original intention, see how far she could be culpable. It's a traitorous, treacherous proceeding; but, for Herbert's sake, I must go through with it.

MRS. H. (*rising*) Well, Doctor, you despise me, of course —then, tell me so at once, and leave me to my despair.

Dr. S. Oh! Mrs. Waverley, you may have some reasonable show of vindication, in your sex's proverbial weakness; but, how can I defend myself from reproach, when I confess that, overpowered by a similar infatuation, your words have found but too ready an echo within my disloyal heart? (*aside*) That's not so bad to begin with.

Mrs. H. Doctor!

Mrs. S. What's that? Oh! the false villain; let him proceed, and let's see how far he'll go.

Dr. S. (*aside*) I don't know whether that's the right sort of thing or not; but it's as near as I can get to it. (*aloud*) Yes, yes, dear madam, emboldened by your sorrowfully sweet confession, I now declare that your sentiments are reciprocated ardently, devotedly, desperately. (*aside*) There's nothing like going it strong while you're about it.

Mrs. H. (*starting up*) Oh, this is infamous—see what you have exposed me to. (*aside to* Mrs. Savage)

Mrs. S. But, think of me—patience, for my sake. Oh! the hypocritical profligate.

Dr. S. And therefore if your love be as strong as mine, and you would fain break the bonds that keep us from each other, let us fly at once.

Mrs. H. Fly, sir; where?

Dr. S. Anywhere—everywhere—the farther off the better.

Mrs. H. But your wife, sir;—she who is so entirely devoted to you!

Dr. S. Oh! ah! yes; I didn't think of her; but never mind, she'll be glad enough to get rid of me.

Mrs. H. Perhaps she may. How soon would you be prepared to go?

Dr. S. Well, that's matter-of-fact enough—I wonder if she really would fly! I'll see—suppose we say to-morrow.

Mrs. H. Very well, sir, I shall meet you here.

Exit, l. 2 e.

Dr. S. She will fly—good gracious! oh! I must put a sudden stop to this disgraceful affair. Madam, allow me to decline—(*turns*) oh! she's gone. Oh! my poor deeply injured friend, what a task have I to perform—but it must be done at once, whatever the result. Why did I undertake it, and what on earth am I to say to Herbert? that

his wife has an insane passion for another, and that other—
but I'd better keep that to myself, why should I tell him
anything at all about it? I must—I must—honor—friendship—propriety demand it. Oh! woman—woman—what
an inscrutable riddle thou art!   *Exit*, c.

Enter MRS. HERBERT *and* MRS. SAVAGE, L. *door.*

MRS. H. My poor dear Fanny.

MRS. S. Oh! don't come near me—I hate you. (*crosses
to* L.) Oh! my darling dear good soul, isn't this shocking.
Oh! if I only had a brother, or even a cousin—but I'll
never see him again!—never, never!

MRS. H. I confess, dear, I am both pained and surprised. You must be satisfied that by no look or word of
mine have I given him the slightest encouragement.

MRS. S. But he might have kept his guilty passion
buried in his own false heart if you hadn't been so un-
necessarily affectionate.

MRS. H. Was it not at your own desire?

MRS. S. Yes, yes, I was to blame, and now I'm miserable, for, in spite of what I said to you, I do love him.
Oh! I was most ungrateful. I didn't know the extent of
my happiness until I find it stripped from me so suddenly,
but won't I punish him for it.

HERB. (*without*) Just gone, you say?

MRS. S. Ah, here's your husband, I'll let him know
what a traitor he has nursed in his bosom.

MRS. H. Be careful, Fanny, remember what consequences may ensue.

MRS. S. I don't care for consequences now.
                              Exit MRS. HERBERT, R. 2. E.

Enter HERBERT, C.

MRS. S. (R.) Oh, Mr. Waverly, I have something
dreadful to tell you.

HERB. My wife?

MRS. S. No, no! I'm in such a temper! Promise me
that you'll be cool, and above all things, that you won't
take any desperate step, no matter what I have to
communicate?

HERB. I promise.

MRS. S. Oh, sir, I have made such a heartrending

discovery; prepare yourself to receive tidings of horror—
nerve yourself to listen to a tale of deceit and treachery—
your friend, my husband, is a traitor, false both to you
and me.

HERB. Indeed, how so pray?

MRS. S. In one frightful sentence, he loves your wife!

HERB. (*aside*) Ah! I understand. (*aloud*) Is it possible,
why you really do surprise me.

MRS. S. It doesn't appear as though I did, sir—do you
understand what I say?

HERB. Perfectly; you say that your husband is in love
with my wife. What led you to imagine so?

MRS. S. The evidence of my own senses—I heard him
avow it here, on this spot, a few minutes ago.

HERB. How very wrong of him.

MRS. S. Oh, you think it's wrong of him, do you.

HERB. Very, not to have made himself certain that
there were no inconvenient listeners to his declaration.
However I am extremely obliged to you, for having
given me the interesting information, and rest assured I
shall take the earliest opportunity of letting him know
my appreciation of his conduct.

MRS. S. Mr. Waverly, this show of indifference cannot be real, it is put on to deceive me, you must have a
more serious purpose at heart. The fierceness of my
passion is now subdued by a dread of something to come,
I have your promise—can I depend upon it, you will not
suffer your vengeance to fall on him.

HERB. Have no fear, my dear madam, whatever be the
result, he will be safe.

MRS. S. Oh, I thank you a thousand times, for though
I shall never see him again, I could not endure the thought
that my rash words had wrought him mischief.

DR. S. (*without*) I must see him, only for a moment.

MRS. S. Oh, the false reprobate!   *Rushes out*, R. 2 E.

Enter DOCTOR SAVAGE, C.

DR. S. (R.) Hollo! wasn't that Fanny?

HERB. Yes—by some unlucky chance she overheard
your interview with my wife.

DR. S. All of it?

HERB. That I don't know.

DR. S. Oh, then I see she didn't.

HERB. (*laughing*) I'm afraid, William, I have got you into something of a scrape.

DR. S. He calls it a scrape—don't laugh, my dear Herbert. (*aside*) How can I break it to him? (*aloud*) Don't laugh, Herbert, you have my sincere pity; bear it like a man.

HERB. What do you mean?

DR. S. You know I told you I'd try and find out the cause of your wife's disquiet.

HERB. Yes—yes—go on.

DR. S. Don't be impetuous—call up all your philosophy.

HERB. Don't keep me on the rack!

DR. S. Imagine the worst, my poor dear friend; and the reality far exceeds it. It was a painful duty, Herbert; but it is done.

HERB. She has then an affection for another? miserable wretch that I am. (*going to* L.)

DR. S. Yes, and miserable wretch that I am. (*going to* R.)

HERB. Who is the scoundrel?

DR. S. There's no scoundrel, Herbert, he doesn't—I mean he didn't know anything about it; it's a disease, an insanity; there's no necessity for you to know who the fellow is; it wouldn't do you any good, or me either.

HERB. But I must, I insist——

DR. S. I won't tell you.

Enter MRS. SAVAGE, *and* MRS. HERBERT, R. 2 E.

MRS. S. I will—I have told him—oh, double traitor, as Julia herself can bear me witness.

DR. S. No, no—don't be so mad!

MRS. H. Since I am called upon, I must confess it was—

DR. S. Foolish woman, silence!

HERB. William, explain this.

DR. S. I can't—I won't.

HERB. Have you deceived me?

DR. S. No, no—it's all a mistake.

MRS. S. *and* MRS. H. Yes, yes.

DR. S. Serves me right—confound it, you're all mad.

(*as they go up, the Drop descends, and*

END OF THE THIRD ACT.

ACT IV.

SCENE.—*Dr. Savage's, as before.*

Enter PINCHBECK, L. C.

PINCH. All right, he's off for a couple of hours, and so I shall take the liberty of borrowing his coat and his character for a short time (*puts on morning gown*) Egad it's lucky that my elderly pigeon is a little tardy in her flight. Ah! there's no profession without its anxieties. Our doctor's looking somewhat gloomy this morning; domestic sun under a cloud, evidently. My expected visitor appears to be an eligible party. I must investigate the pecuniary. If that should stand the test favourably, I couldn't do better than sacrifice myself—if not, why she'll do for my rustic Romeo. (*bell rings*) Ah! there she is. I must receive her in an imposing attitude.

Enter PERKINS, L. C.

PINCH. Oh! it's you is it.

PERK. Yes, it's me. I've just run over to see how we are getting on.

PINCH. Gloriously. I have a magnificent nibble for you.

PERK. You don't say so. Young and rich?

PINCH. Both, I believe, but you shall see him bye-and-bye. Is the wardrobe comatable to-day.

PERK. (L.) We couldn't have a better chance. Missus keeps to her own room; master's gone out in the blues, and the whole house is blind and deaf.

PINCH. (R.) All the better for us; so you just borrow one of the handsomest dresses you can find, and then come over here. I'll manage to pave the way for you, so that you'll have nothing to do but listen to the voice of love. (*bell*) Ah! that's one of my visitors; don't be alarmed, it's a lady pigeon this time.

Enter WIDOW CRABSTICKE, L. C.

PINCH. You can go, Mary, and don't let me be disturbed upon any account.

PERK. No, sir.   *Exit*, C.

PINCH. (R.) Take a seat, madam—you'll excuse me while I write a prescription. (*writes*)

MRS. C. (L., *sits down on a sofa*) Oh! certainly, sir. Pray proceed in your estimable vocation; from the appearance of things it seems to be more profitable than praiseworthy.

PINCH. (L. *of* R., *table*) I must confess, madam, that it *is* profitable, painfully profitable to a naturally well-balanced mind; but, my dear lady, you mustn't be too hard upon those who are driven into such crooked ways by the sharp punctures of necessity; added to which, you should recollect that if there were no market for contraband articles the smuggling fraternity would be crushed out.

MRS. C. Yes, that's very true, and while there are perverse minds to hunger after forbidden fruit, serpents will never be wanted to shew where it can be found.

PINCH. Precisely, madam; the comparison is not flattering, but the metaphor is undeniable.

MRS. C. I'm glad, sir, you have decency enough to acknowledge it.

PINCH. Oh! I'm a man of the world, madam, and know exactly the value of its opinion.

MRS. C. Well, sir, I have not come here for argument, but business.

PINCH. Quite aware of that fact, madam, and admire equally your frankness and freedom of speech, so to business. (MRS. C. *rises and goes to chair* L. *of* R. *table.* PINCHBECK *gets round to chair* R. *of* R. *table*) Let us go at once. How shall I designate you on my books?

MRS. C. What do you mean, sir?

PINCH. What name do you choose to be known by?

MRS. C. Why my own, sir, of course; but I don't see the necessity for parading it.

PINCH. Certainly not, madam, it wouldn't be advisable; suppose we say Juliet.

MRS. C. Juliet. Why Juliet? I don't exactly understand.

PINCH. Matter of delicacy, that is all. (*aside*) Now for the needful—hem! Name Juliet. (*writing*) Appearance elegant. Property? Sad, but certain that folks *will*

make so small a matter—point of particular inquiry.
Mingles as naturally with the affections as green leaves
among the orange blossoms.   May I venture to ask how
we are situated with regard to the despicable dross.

Mrs. C. (*aside*) The fellow's afraid of his fee. (*aloud*)
Don't be under any apprehension, sir; only bring this
affair to a termination quickly, and demand what you
please.

Pinch. (*aside*) Rich, I think; but, I mustn't be in a
hurry. (*aloud*) And now, madam, for the most important
consideration of all, as far as you are personally concerned.

Mrs. C. What may that be, sir?

Pinch. Have you any particular predilection with regard to age, profession, country, or characteristics?

Mrs. C. Why should I?

Pinch. No reason in the world, madam—leaves me free
to do the best I can for you.

Mrs. C. I'm delighted to hear it.   Use your own discretion, and, for gracious sake, let there be no delay.

Pinch. The Fates are propitious—I have a certain
Romeo on my books. (*both rise*)

Mrs. C. That's the very man I want.

Pinch. Indeed, madam—pleasing coincidence—I expect him every moment.   If he should consent, as of
course he will, the whole affair can be settled at once.

Mrs. C. (L.) It shall be settled, sir, whether he consent or not; he shan't escape me.   No, no, I'll take him
back with me, if I have to be bound to him hand and foot.

Pinch. (*aside*) I've heard of hands and hearts being
bound together, but I don't know what the feet have to
do with it—very determined old lady this. (*bell rings*)
Ah, that must be our man.   Hadn't I better prepare him
for the tender meeting?

Mrs. C. I don't care, sir; just as you please, so that
secure him for me before I leave the house.

Pinch. I'll do my best.   Will you please to step into
this room, and at the proper moment I shall have the
extreme felicity of bringing you together.

Mrs. C. Never, I trust, to be separated.   *Exit*, R. 2 E.

Pinch. Fallacious hope! but that's no affair of mine;
this Romeo must be a bird worth the catching; some

D

young fledgling, I suppose, she has set her antediluvian heart upon. (*goes and sits in arm chair*, L. *of* R. *table*)

Enter UNCLE TIMOTHY, C.

PINCH. Hollo! who's this?

UNCLE T. Hush. Are you Doctor Savage?

PINCH. At your service, sir.

UNCLE T. All right—how-d'ye-do?—I'm Romeo.

PINCH. Oh! you *are*, are you? (*aside*) My preconceived notions slightly exaggerated.

UNCLE T. Yes, I'm Romeo—you saw the item in the paper. Bless me, I'm as nervous as a school-boy—you're sure we're quite safe here, nobody to overhear us.

PINCH. Quite, sir. Everything conducted in this office with the most honourable secrecy.

UNCLE T. This seems to be a strange way to procure a wife, sir; but the fact is, I really never could muster up courage enough to make any advances myself.

PINCH. Don't be in the remotest degree embarrassed, my dear sir; it's my pleasant duty to interpose a brazen shield before the most diffident.

UNCLE T. Exactly—so I thought. You got my last letter?

PINCH. With a satisfactory enclosure, in due course.

UNCLE T. Well, and have you seen anything suitable? I don't care much about money, but youth and beauty are indispensable?

PINCH. Of course. (*aside*) I'm afraid my elderly Juliet is out of the question; I'll try him with Perkins.

UNCLE T. You have seen somebody then?

PINCH. The very individual you desire.

UNCLE T. Describe her.

PINCH. Eighteen years old, plump as a spring chicken, sweet-tempered as a summer zephyr, graceful as a young gazelle, and accomplished as a college professor.

UNCLE T. That will do—my style exactly—phew! I feel a glow of happiness in advance, as new as it's delicious. But do you think she'll like me enough to share my fortune?

PINCH. I'll answer for that—with *my* assistance.

UNCLE T. Enough—I'll never forget you.

PINCH. I don't think you will.

UNCLE T. But when can I see her?

PINCH. Before many minutes elapse I expect her here.

UNCLE T. You do—phew! There's a rush of something not quite so pleasurable; I'm almost afraid that I've been too hasty. (*bell rings*)

·PINCH. That must be she! Now, sir, prepare for beauty irresistible!

UNCLE T. I will.

DR. S. (*without*) Put the horse up, I shan't go out again just at present.

PINCH. It's the Doctor, as I'm an undone negotiator. My dear sir, it's one of my very particular patients come at rather an unreasonable hour. I presume you wouldn't like to be seen here by any one?

UNCLE T. No, no, not for the world—put me somewhere until he is gone.

PINCH. Just step in here. (*crossing*, L.) As soon as I can I shall get rid of him.

UNCLE TIMOTHY *goes into room*, L. 1 E.

PINCH. (*takes off gown and cap*) Was ever anything so *malapropos?* Confound it, what brought him back so soon?

Enter DR. SAVAGE, C., *takes off coat, flings it to* PINCHBECK, *then puts on dressing gown and cap.*

DR. S. This coat's warm, has anybody been wearing it?

PINCH. No, it felt damp, and I put it before the fire.

DR. S. A decidedly pleasant hornet's nest I have thrust my head into, upon my soul! Fanny developes a beautiful new phase in her character which I have hitherto been unaware of, and exhibits a supernatural jealousy. I hadn't the remotest idea I was so inconveniently fascinating. As for Mrs. Waverly, her anger was, of course, assumed, to blind poor Herbert; and even he appeared half inclined to reproach me for having for friendship's sake made the unfortunate discovery which has brought confusion and unhappiness to us all.

PINCH. (*aside*) Something wrong somewhere. How the deuce shall I get my pigeon away?

DR. S. Oh! by-the-bye, Pinchbeck, I had almost forgotten—be so good as to take this prescription, and have it made up.

PINCH. (*aside*) Phew!—here's a precious mess. (*aloud*) Yes, sir. (*aside*) It's not far; I must trust to luck, and hurry back. Oh! what's to become of my pigeon? *Exit*, C.

DR. S. This comes of endeavouring to serve a friend. I wish the meddling demon that suggested it to me had stayed at home.

Enter HERBERT, C.

DR. S. Ah! Herbert, is that you? (*offers his hand*)

HERB. (*refusing*) Excuse me, one moment, if you please. You must be aware that I am entitled to an explanation?

DR. S. Confound it, haven't I explained enough for a man of a retiring temperament? what would you have more?

HERB. The truth, the definite and entire truth. Both your wife and mine intimated blame on your part, although without exactly mentioning particulars.

DR. S. My wife is a jealous little fool, and yours——

HERB. Well, and mine——

DR. S. Is a greater fool of another sort.

HERB. This is too vague and unsatisfactory; if I cannot induce you as a friend to disclose all you know, I have at least the right to demand it from you as a man.

DR. S. Good gracious, how obtuse you are! Can't you estimate the delicacy which prevents me from entering into further details about this unfortunate affair? Didn't I tell you——

HERB. That she had a secret affection for another.

DR. S. Precisely.

HERB. But for whom?

DR. S. Why, for me—for me; there now, I hope you're satisfied that you have no cause for fear.

HERB. And do you dare tell me that such a feeling could be nurtured and perpetuated without some advances upon your part?

DR. S. Herbert!

HERB. Oh, don't look absurdly indignant at me! it's the usual part played by the wily profligate—the hectoring bluster, which is the only resource left to the discovered traitor.

DR. S. Now I'm a wily profligate and a discovered traitor, Herbert; if I thought it were *you*, and not your unreflecting anger that spoke, I would be more inclined to resent the calumny; but as it is, I shall leave you to get cool again. (*going*)

HERB. Stay; do you assure me solemnly that you never gave her encouragement.

DR. S. The thought is offensive, but in pity to your distress of mind, I answer no—unequivocally no!

HERB. She has *not* visited you then?

DR. S. This is irritating and most unjustifiable. Your wife has never been here without you.

HERB. William, I *must* believe you; but think, oh, think of the fiery shame that so consumes me, that madness would be merciful! I'll see you soon again, when I shall be better able to consult with you what step I had better take. *Exit*, C.

DR. S. Now, the deuce take the woman and her preposterous passion; she's likely to give me trouble enough.

Enter UNCLE TIMOTHY *from chamber*, L.

UNCLE T. I say, friend, isn't she a long time coming?

DR. S. (*aside*) Who, on earth, is this? Why, as I live, it's her uncle—what does he want?—he doesn't know me. (*aloud*) Of whom do you speak, sir?

UNCLE T. Hush! the lady you expect.

DR. S. It can't be possible Mrs. Waverly meditates such a fearful proceeding—is she coming here?

UNCLE T. Of course—why you know she is—is he gone?

DR. S. Yes, just gone.

UNCLE T. I'm glad of it, then we're alone, ain't we?

DR. S. Quite alone.

UNCLE T. Well then, let us come to an understanding, you had better make some arrangement with her, yourself; I don't think I could have courage to meet her just now. If she's what *you* say, and you know best about that —couldn't you manage to keep her here for a few days?

DR. S. Keep her here? what are you talking about? No, sir, I must beg leave to decline that proposition, it's utterly impossible—egad, I've had trouble enough about her already.

UNCLE T. Well, sir, suppose you have, I'll indemnify you amply; but you must place her somewhere for the present, I don't want my nephew to know anything about it, until we are gone.

DR. S. Then permit me to say, you are too late, for he knows everything about it already.

UNCLE T. Indeed!

DR. S. Yes, I told him all.

UNCLE T. I'm very much obliged to you, and how did he take it?

DR. S. Very indignantly; he's in a terrible rage.

UNCLE T. Yes, of course, I thought he would; but we can't help that now.

DR. S. Eh! why isn't this—yes, by all that's reckless, she's here now, and closely veiled. I wash my hands of it, come to what conclusion you may, I'll have no more to do with the matter.

UNCLE T. My dear sir, you mustn't do that, after bringing us into this embarrassing position.

DR. S. I, bring you into it?

UNCLE T. Yes, you—hang it, man, at least be honest to your villanies; don't shrink from the consequences of your own disreputable act.

DR. S. Why, you don't believe——

UNCLE T. Stuff! I know all about it—here she comes, I rely upon you to manage it all, if I can collect myself sufficiently, I shall come out of my hiding place, if not, all you have to do is to settle where we can meet. *Exit*, L. 1 E.

DR. S. Good heavens! I'm in a maze of astonishment and apprehension; can this imprudent woman, blinded by her mad love for me, have taken so desperate a step, and Fanny even now devoured by a false jealousy—what would she say if—oh, I can't! I won't! I must be firm!

Enter PERKINS, C., *in Mrs. Waverly's dress.*

PERK. (*down*, R.) Well, is he come?

DR. S. Madam, this can no longer be endured. Your partiality though flattering is confoundedly inconvenient, and—(*sees her face*) That face—it isn't she; but I'll swear to her dress—who are you. (*turns her round*) Hollo! are you not Mrs. Waverly's waiting woman?

PERK. (*crying*) Yes, sir; I confess I am—forgive me, sir, and I'll tell you everything.

DR. S. You'll oblige me very materially if you do. Come, come, don't be alarmed—sit down. (*aside*) Perhaps I may hear something consolatory. (*aloud*) Well, go on.

PERK. (*crying*) Oh, sir, I have acted so wickedly, I'm afraid you'll never forgive me.

DR. S. Well, don't cry—hang it! a woman's tears are too much for my stoicism—there—there, I won't be angry, if you only speak the truth.

PERK. (*crying*) I will, sir, as soon as I ca—can; but I'm so overcome with your goodness.

DR. S. Confound it woman, stop whimpering, and tell me what you've done.

Enter PINCHBECK, L. C.

PINCH. (*aside*) I thought so—it's all up with us, what's to be done? By jingo! here comes Mrs. Savage, it's a dreadful chance. (*aloud*) Hem! Doctor!

(PERKINS *faints in* DOCTOR SAVAGE'S *arms*)

PINCH. Take care. (*makes signs of caution*) I thought you wouldn't like anybody to discover.

Enter MRS. SAVAGE, C.

DR. S. For gracious sake, don't make a scene. Lord—Lord—if Fanny were to see this.

Enter HERBERT, L. C.

MRS. S. (*confronting them*) She does see it, traitor!

PERKINS *screams, and runs off*, L. C.

HERB. Why, Julia! isn't that my wife?

PINCH. I regret to be compelled to say, it is.

HERB. Well, sir, how will you contrive to twist yourself out of this disgraceful predicament?

DR. S. Herbert, I—don't you know.

MRS. S. You don't expect I'm going to remain under your good-for-nothing roof?

DR. S. What is the matter with you both?

MRS. S. Oh, dear, Mr. Waverly, what is to become of me? (*crosses to* HERBERT, L., *and throws herself into his arms*)

DR. S. That's pleasant!

HERB. My dear madam, I can but too truly sympathize with you.

DR. S. Fanny!

MRS. S. Oh, don't speak to me.

HERB. William, be assured, you shall atone dearly for your treacherous conduct.

DR. S. Well, this is refreshing, he hugs my wife up in his arms, and threatens me with his vengeance—this is too much for patient endurance, what perverse devil possesses you all?

Enter UNCLE TIMOTHY, L. 1 E.

UNCLE T. Well, friend, have you paved the way for me? She has arrived, I see.

Enter WIDOW CRABSTICKE, R. 2 E.

MRS. C. Yes, she has!

UNCLE T. Oh, law! it's you, is it?

DR. S. Hollo! who's this?

MRS. C. Yes, it's me; are you not ashamed to look me in the face?

UNCLE T. (*to* DR. SAVAGE) Scoundrel! have you betrayed me? Didn't I bribe you enough to be honest?

MRS. C. No, you didn't, so prepare to come back with me into the country.

UNCLE T. I shall do nothing of the kind.

MRS. C. Oh, this is too much! (*throws herself on* DR. SAVAGE)

DR. S. It is, ma'am, a deuced deal too much. (*pushes her over to* UNCLE TIMOTHY, *who flings her into a chair*)

MRS. S. Oh, you Giovanni!

HERB. You unprincipled deceiver!

UNCLE T. You treacherous impostor! (PINCHBECK *capers about at back—all denounce the* DOCTOR, *who sinks exhausted into a chair*)

END OF ACT THE FOURTH.

ACT V.

SCENE.—*Apartment at Waverly's.   Case of pistols on table.—Same as Act II.*

HERBERT *discovered sealing a letter.*

HERB. There, my last employment upon earth is done. She shall find, unworthy though she be, that I have not carried my revenge beyond the dark threshold that so soon may separate us. I have here written my forgiveness, though I cannot, will not, speak it. To see her again is now impossible; she will read these lines only when the doom I seek has closed my lips for ever. And now to find some *friend* who will bear this message to him who, of all others, I believed the best entitled to be called by that delusive name—friend! Pah! there's no such thing. How little did I dream that I should ever raise my hand in enmity against that man, and for such a cause. Oh! woman, woman! (*buries his face in his hands and leans on the table, so as to be concealed from the C. door*)

Enter PERKINS *cautiously,* C.

PERK. It's all settled. I'm to be married at last; Pinchbeck has managed it beautifully—but I must borrow a little more finery for the occasion.

Goes into side door, L. 2 E.

HERB. (*catching a view as she enters, starts up, looks after her*) See where the detected traitress skulks away; my indignation almost chokes me.

Enter MRS. HERBERT, R. 2 E., *and sits at the table which* HERBERT *has just quitted.*

HERB. The baseness of her conduct utterly destroys the sole touch of weakness that lingered in my heart. Why should I leave a record that would stamp me fool as well as—— (*turns suddenly, rushing towards table as if to destroy the letter—sees* MRS. HERBERT) Julia! who was it entered that room?

MRS. H. I know not. Herbert, what is this? (*points to pistol case*)

HERB. Nothing, no matter. I'm so confused at seeing
you when—was it my heated imagination, or does my
brain give way indeed.

MRS. H. (*firmly*) Herbert, your pistols are here, perhaps I have no right to force an explanation, but, in pity,
dear husband, banish the suspense in which I live ; I
think now that I could bear the worst, even the avowal,
but it must be from your own lips—that I have outlived
your regard. I care not what becomes of me—cast me
off, if you so will it—but, in mercy, break this cruel
silence.

HERB. (*aside, walking away*) Cast her off—she wishes
it—I see she does—it's a subtle stratagem to fling the
odium upon me. Well, be it so—yes, she shall have her
way, and I alone be the sufferer. Julia, be it as you wish,
the bonds which have become so irksome I release you
from ; henceforward you are free.

MRS. H. (*aside*) Oh ! it is hard now to dissemble, but it
is for his sake. Herbert! I submit to my fate.

HERB. Submit ! do you not desire it?

MRS. H. Yes ! yes ! dear husband, if you wish it I am
ready to depart. (*crosses, L.*)

HERB. And no regret—not one reluctant thought?

MRS. H. (*aside*) He can ask that question. Changed—
changed indeed—may you be happy, Herbert.

HERB. Cold, cruel, heartless woman, go. (*she goes towards
door*, L. 2 E.) She will—she will ! Julia, have you no fear
for the unhappy future? not a sigh for the brief blissful
past? is it thus that *we* should part? give me at least one
moment to remember, without grief and indignation.

MRS. H. (*falling into his arms*) Oh ! Herbert, husband,
save me from myself.

Enter UNCLE TIMOTHY, C.

UNCLE T. Aha! that's as it should be. Don't mind
me, I'll soon have an equal privilege. It's all arranged, my
boy—the Doctor managed it for me—gave old she-griffin
the slip, and we've had a glorious lunch together—lots of
champagne, old fellow—turtle soup and brandy punch ;—
by Jove, I think the last spoonful was a little too rich.
Congratulate me, I'm going to be married, you'll have a

surprise sooner than you expect—it strengthens my resolution to see you so. (*looks alternately at each other*) Eh !
God bless me—I'm afraid. I say, Herbert, was it the
effect of the soup, or didn't I see you in each other's
arms? and now, you'll excuse the remark, but I never saw
such a melancholy-looking couple of kill-joys. Julia,
you've been crying, and hang me if I don't think there has
been something moist on your eyes too. Dear me—dear
me—I wish I had reflected a little longer.

HERB. Uncle, it may as well be known at once, prepare
yourself for the worst intelligence I have ever had to
communicate; after so many years of happiness, we are
about to separate.

UNCLE T. Good gracious, you're joking! I won't
believe it, I can't, it's ridiculous, Julia !

MRS. H. It is but too true, dear uncle, I have not
strength to bear up longer against this trial. *Exit*, L. 2 E.

UNCLE T. Oh, well, see here ! this is atrocious, unexpected and horrible; what a fortunate thing it is that I'm
not married yet!

HERB. Into your hands, dear uncle, I confide this paper,
it makes full provision for her future life.

UNCLE T. I won't take it, I decline the responsibility.

HERB. Nay, I have a yet more friendly service, that
you alone can perform. You cannot but perceive that a
painful crisis has arisen, for which there is no alternative
but that. (*touching pistol case*)

UNCLE T. And what may that be ? (*opens case*) Bless
my soul, pistols ! (*falls into chair*, R.)

HERB. I have been dishonoured, uncle; tricked, gulled,
my unsuspicious confidence abused, despoiled of that a
thousand lives could not atone for.

UNCLE. You surprise and terrify me, my dear boy, you
surely can't mean that Julia, your wife ? (*he nods*) My
goodness, who could have dreamt of such a thing ! and
I, blind, unthinking simpleton as I was—(*crosses to* L.)
I mean, what must I do ?

HERB. You must take this letter and deliver it in
person. (*gives letter*)

UNCLE T. What is it ?

HERB. A challenge.

UNCLE T. What, a duel?

HERB. Yes, and you must act as my second.

UNCLE T. You're not serious, Herbert? Why, I never saw a pistol fired in my life.

HERB. So much the better.

UNCLE T. But who is it? (*reads*) Eh, what? bless me! Doctor Savage, is he the fellow?

HERB. Yes, do you know him?

UNCLE T. Know him? I should think so—for as mischievous and unprincipled a rascal as ever lived on lies.

HERB. Can this be possible?

UNCLE. T. Not only possible, but true, as I to my shame can testify.

HERB. What do you mean, Uncle?

UNCLE. I mean that his office is a surreptitious marriage mart—a convenient rendezvous where shy Cupids may borrow confidence. I don't mind confessing to you it was this reprobate who smoothed my matrimonial pathway; but, thank my good fortune, the sacrifice is not completed, though I presume I'll have to risk a " breach of promise case." But, no matter; better to pay in cash than comfort.

HERB. Vile, treacherous hypocrite. Uncle, I am ashamed to ask you to carry my message to so despicable a fellow; but there's no alternative.

UNCLE. Herbert, I'll do it.

HERB. Thanks, my good friend—and at once.

Exit, R. 2 E.

UNCLE T. Hang me if I wouldn't like to have a pop at the scoundrel myself!

Enter PINCHBECK, C., *he touches* TIMOTHY *on the shoulder.*

PINCH. Well, old boy, I've been looking out for you!

UNCLE T. Have you? then you've saved me a good deal of trouble, for I was just going to look out for you.

PINCH. How lucky it is we met—it's all right, I've found a friend to officiate.

UNCLE. T. I'm glad of it; then you anticipate my business?

PINCH. Certainly, we shall be ready in about half an hour.

UNCLE T. Well, the sooner the better, though I must say, you take it coolly; I wonder you have the daring impudence to shew yourself beneath this roof.

PINCH. I wouldn't, but to tell you the truth, *she's* here.

UNCLE T. I know she is.

PINCH. Have you seen her?

UNCLE T. I have, sir, and also the bitter consequence of your rascality in her misery and tears.

PINCH. (*aside*) Tears—oh, the artful baggage. (*aloud*) All humbug, my. dear sir—don't mind that—put on for effect—she'll be happy enough by-and-bye.

UNCLE T. How so?

PINCH. Why, didn't she tell you that we had made arrangements to leave the house together?

UNCLE T. Oh you have, have you?

PINCH. Yes; I expect the carriage at the end of the street shortly. She is quietly to steal out of the house, then off we are all together on the road to happiness.

UNCLE T. (*aside*) Well, of all the audacious rascals I ever heard of, this icy-hearted vagabond is the most uncompromising. (*aloud*) And, pray sir, where do you mean to take her?

PINCH. That, of course, rests with yourself.

UNCLE. With me?

PINCH. Certainly. You'll take her with you into the country, I presume. What fitter place than your own house?

UNCLE T. My house—why, man, you're crazy.

PINCH. Well, perhaps it would be more judicious to remain somewhere quietly until the little irregularity blows over.

UNCLE T. (*aside*) Phew! he calls his gigantic crime a little irregularity; pah! I can have no more words with such a cold-blooded ruffian. Sir, I don't know what indication of villany in my countenance prompted you to make me your confidant, but this I *do* know, that our family is under an amount of obligation to you which I sincerely trust this document will fully discharge. (*gives letter*)   *Exit,* c.

PINCH. Singular old fellow that; it isn't often that people abuse the means, however questionable, through

E

which they are assisted. What have we here, I wonder?
A handsome remuneration for my invaluable services, no
doubt!

Enter MRS. CRABSTICKE, C.

MRS. C. There he is! (*down*, R.)

PINCH. It will be a fine stroke of matrimonial diplomacy.

MRS. C. (*seizing the letter*) You'll excuse me, sir, if I
deem it necessary to put a stop to your disgraceful diplomacy, at least, in the present instance. .

PINCH. But, my dear madam, this does not appertain
to your business at all, which, I am happy to say, is
progressing most favourably.

MRS. C. Hold your tongue. (*reads*) What's here—a
challenge? did my brother give you this?

PINCH. Your brother, madam? I have not the pleasure
of his acquaintance.

MRS. C. I mean he who quitted the room just now.

PINCH. Yes, ma'am, he did; but I really wasn't aware—

MRS. C. Ah! well, I don't want to interfere with any
arrangement of this kind.

PINCH. I'm glad to hear it, madam, and am quite
certain it will be a great comfort to your brother, to know
that you have no objection.

MRS. C. It's nothing to me, though how he came to be
mixed up in such a matter, I can't imagine.

PINCH. Without undue flattery, I think I may say, *I*
brought it about rather cleverly, too, and I should be
most happy to negotiate a similar affair for you. ·

MRS. C. Don't be impertinent, sir. (*crosses to* R. *and sits*)

PINCH. (*examining letter*) What on earth is this?
" imfamous treachery!—satisfaction!—wrongs avenged!"
A deadly challenge—now whether this is for me, or my
reputable double, I'll be hanged if I can tell.

DR. S. (*without*, C.) Come along, and don't bother. 1
tell you, I shan't sleep without an explanation.

PINCH. Hollo! here he is!

Enter DR. SAVAGE *and* MRS. SAVAGE.

DR. S. Why, Pinchbeck, what are you doing here?

MRS. C. Pinchbeck!

PINCH. (*aside to* MRS. CRABSTICKE) Hush! a nickname
—tell you all bye-and-bye, if you'll only please to go now.

MRS. C. But I don't please to go now, sir, I please to
stay and frustrate your nefarious intentions.

DR. S. What's all this?

PINCH. (*aside*) I have it. (*aloud*) Madam, you are
right, they must be frustrated. (*to* DR. SAVAGE) May I
say a word to you alone, sir?

DR. S. To be sure—Fanny, go and find Mrs. Waverly,
and depend upon what I have promised.

MRS. S. I wish I could; but you are such an adept at
deception—I'm afraid to indulge the hope. *Exit*, L. 2 E.

DR. S. Now, sir, what have you to say to me?

PINCH. In a word, sir, have you cause to fear a hostile
message from any party?

DR. S. Hostile message? No!

PINCH. Not from Mr. Waverly?

DR. S. Has he proceeded to so ridiculous an extremity?

PINCH. He has, sir.

DR. S. Then he's madder than I thought he was.

PINCH. I obtained knowledge of the fact, and in my
anxiety for your safety took the liberty of intercepting
the document—here it is. The bearer of this not knowing
you, I, following an irresistible impulse, told him I was
Dr. Savage, in the hope of averting so great a calamity,
if necessary, by the sacrifice of myself.

DR. S. You have been very considerate, I must say;
but, don't be alarmed, there will be no necessity for any
such exhibition of disinterested bravery—all will be
settled when I see Herbert.

PINCH. I need not say how rejoiced I am at this information; but, pray, sir, if any one should mention my
assumption of your name, remember the motive and
pardon the impertinence.

DR. S. To be sure, Pinchbeck; but, run to the office,
there's no one there.

PINCH. At once, sir. (*to* MRS. C.) If you would avert a
great calamity, follow me.

MRS. C. You may depend upon it, sir, you don't quit
my sight again I promise you.

Exeunt PINCHBECK *and* MRS. C., C.

DR. S. A most delicious entanglement I've managed
to establish by consenting to that absurd proposition.
Fanny is suffering under a savage attack of jealousy, and
to appease her I must now inform this poor woman, who
has, heaven knows how, conceived so violent a passion
for me, that she must be content to pine in misery, as, of
course, she will—ah, here they both come; stern duty
triumphs over delicacy—phychologic surgery should be
sharp and decided.

Enter MRS. SAVAGE *and* MRS. HERBERT, R. C.

MRS. S. Now, sir, here is Julia; be good enough to
commence your explanation.

DR. S. Hem! believe me, my dear madam, I regret to
witness your distress; but domestic comfort is superior to
small sacrifices, and the unworthy image which has obtained a place within your heart must be obliterated.   It
may cost you a pang—no doubt it will—but in the end
we shall all be the happier for it.

MRS. H. You ask for an impossibility.   Never, sir, can
I banish that beloved image from my heart.

MRS. S. There, sir.

DR. S. What, madam, when I tell you emphatically
that this ridiculous passion is not in the remotest degree
reciprocated?

MRS. H. It well becomes you, my husband's friend, to
tell me that.

DR. S. Confound it, madam, it's because I *am* his friend
I'm forced to be thus explicit.

MRS. H. I know it, sir, but have you never had one
thought for me?

DR. S. Never, madam, never! I do assure you, upon
my honor, I regret to appear so cruel, but it's always best
to have a definite understanding.

MRS. H. Enough, sir! If you are capable of making
so cold-hearted an avowal at such a crisis, in simple duty
to myself I must decline your further acquaintance.

DR. S. Madam, I can't say that I regret the decision
you have come to.

MRS. H. Very well, sir, be it so—you shall find that I
have sufficient pride to sustain me—even in this trial of

my fortitude and temper—and however my husband's alienated love may fill my after life with sorrow, it cannot equal the contempt and scorn with which I shall remember one who, dead to every principle of honor or humanity, adds thus the crowning grief to my great misery. (*goes up and sits*, L.)

DR. S. Well, upon my life and soul, this is sufficiently refrigerating—you seem to forget, madam, that my wife is present.

MRS. S. Pray don't mind me,

MRS. H. What (*coming down*, L.) has that to do with it?

MRS. S. Certainly, what has that to do with it? I'm nobody, so don't take the trouble to dissemble any more, but tell the truth, although you shame each other.

DR. S. Truth! what do you mean? haven't I——

MRS. S. It's no use trying to deceive me any longer, I know you have both been secretly attached.

MRS. H. Fanny!

MRS. S. Oh! nonsense! didn't I overhear your affectionate conversation?

MRS. H. Which you advised.

DR. S. What's that?

MRS. S. Yes, but I didn't imagine I was using my breath to rekindle an old fire.

DR. S. Oh, it was you advised that interesting conversation, eh? I do believe I begin to see a bit of blue sky! You don't mean to say that your sudden *penchant* for me was a sham?

MRS. H. I do indeed.

DR. S. And you don't nourish a fatal passion for the subscriber within your beautiful anatomy?

MRS. H. Certainly not, sir.

DR. S. You still love Herbert?

MRS. H. Deeply, enduringly.

DR. S. Hurrah, it's all serene—the clouds are clearing away rapidly, I must insist upon embracing you both. Listen: in an unlucky moment, it was agreed between Herbert and me—agitated and distressed at a sorrow which, I must say, you very clumsily endeavoured to conceal, that I should try the self-same mode of treatment suggested by my little woman. I ought to have foreseen the inevitable result, for we always think alike, don't we, dear?

MRS. S. I think you've been a very great fool.

DR. S. So do I, darling—our agreement is as perfect' as ever.

MRS. H. And Herbert, my husband?

DR. S. Has never wavered an instant in his truth and love, to that I'll pledge my life!

MRS. H. Do you indeed assure me of this? Oh, my dear, good friend—I'm so ashamed of my violence.

MRS. S. And I of my suspicion. (*they both embrace* DR. SAVAGE)

Enter HERBERT, R. 2 E., *he starts angrily.*

HERB. What do I behold? (*down*, R.)

DR. S. Sir, you behold the happiest medical practitioner within the bills of mortality, for I have the key to that comfort and domestic felicity which you wilfully locked against yourself.

HERB. What do you mean?

DR. S. I mean that you're cured—cured, both of you. You were suffering from a plethora of comfort, and the depletion has done you good; there, take your wife un-. changed in anything except the anxiety that's gone for ever—but, for gracious sake, don't let us have any more imaginary maladies.

HERB. Julia, can this good news be true?

MRS. H. My loyal heart has never abandoned its allegiance, dear Herbert, even in the midst of traitorous suspicions.

HERB. But tell me——

DR. S. Not now—by-and-bye. Take your wife, and don't ask impertinent questions.

HERB. My dear Julia.

MRS. H. Dear husband.

MRS. S. My dear Doctor. (*they embrace*)

Enter UNCLE TIMOTHY, C.

UNCLE T. Well, Herbert, I delivered the message to that rascally friend of yours, Dr. Savage!

DR. S. I beg your pardon, sir; allow me to say that·

you seem to exhibit a very reckless disregard for historic accuracy.

Uncle T. That, I suppose, is the elegant way of telling a man he lies. Who may you be, sir?

Herb. Uncle, this is Doctor Savage.

Uncle T. This Doctor Savage—I'll be hanged if it is.

Dr. S. Will you?—then you'd better look after the rope, sir, for I certainly am Doctor Savage.

Uncle T. (*showing letter*) You—is this your address?

Dr. S. It is.

Uncle T. Physician?

Dr. S. Yes.

Uncle T. And matrimonial agert?

Dr. S. No!—stop! Could that scamp Pinchbeck have assumed my name for other purposes than that he spoke of?

Uncle T. You may soon have an opportunity of knowing, sir; for the fellow, mistaking the purport of my interview with him, has promised to meet me here almost immediately.

Herb. For what purpose, uncle?

Uncle T. By Jove, I'm ashamed to acknowledge it, but I may as well make a clean breast at once. I was to be married (*all laugh*) to a sweet young creature—quite a lady, I assure you; and more than that, the fellow contrived to gain my sister's consent to be present at the interesting ceremony.

Dr. S. This accounts for the matrimonial agency. Do me the favour to proceed as though such were your intention; meantime we can watch the result from some convenient hiding place.

Mrs. S. I wonder who the lady is.

Herb. Here they both come, I declare.

Dr. S. Then let us keep out of view for the present.

Exeunt all into room, r., *but* Timothy.

Enter Pinchbeck *and* Widow Crabsticke, c.

Pinch. Ah, sir! arrived before me, I perceive.

Uncle T. Yes, my dear doctor—naturally anxious to have this delicate affair settled.

MRS. C. I little thought I should ever find you engaged in such work.

UNCLE T. And I as little expected to find you seconding me in it.

MRS. C. I second you? Don't be an idiot! what are you talking about?

PINCH. May I beg of you to be cautious, and speak low?

MRS. C. Speak low! why should I, sir?

PINCH. You must be aware, my dear madam, that we are engaged in a business which demands secrecy.

MRS. C. I am not, sir, whatever you may be. I only kept in your track to discover him, and now I've done with you, for out of this house he don't go without me—it's a mercy he has escaped so long.

UNCLE T. But suppose I tell you that I have made up my mind to carry out my intentions.

PINCH. Certainly, exercise the prerogative of your sex, we can do without that old tabby; so be firm, take the goods the gods provide you, Romeo, and be happy. (*leading* PERKINS *from room*, R. 3 E.)

MRS. C. A woman! (*all advance from their concealment laughing*)

DR. S. Bravo! well done, Dr. Savage. (PERKINS *endeavours to get away—* DR. SAVAGE *detains her*) One moment, madam, if you please; we must find out who you are. (*takes off veil*)

MRS. H. Perkins, and in my dress!

HERB. Dear, dear Julia, what's the meaning of this?

PERK. Oh! I don't know—it's all Mr. Pinchbeck's fault—he over-persuaded me—said he'd make my fortune by getting me a nice rich husband, if I could only borrow one of missus's dresses.

UNCLE T. Yes, my dear; I was the fortunate individual selected to sustain that fortunate character.

PERK. You, sir! (*to* MRS. HERBERT) Oh, madam, please forgive me, and I'll never think of such a terrible thing again.

MRS. H. Husband?

HERB. Do as you please, darling. I have been been so culpable, but am now so happy, that I am inclined to deal leniently with the mistakes of others.

Mrs. H. Forget the past then, Perkins, and be more prudent in the future.

Perk. That I will, indeed, ma'am, and thank your most grateful—goodness, oh my! what a narrow escape I've had.   *Exit* c., *pushing* Pinchbeck.

(*all go up stage, except* Mrs. Crabsticke *and* Uncle Timothy)

Mrs. C. Well, brother, I hope you have had enough of wife-hunting to last you for the remainder of your life.

Uncle T. By Jove, I have, though I were to outlive Old Parr, himself. For the future, I accept your sisterly rule—look upon me as the ghost of the departed Crabsticke—henceforth, lecture as you may, I'll be as quiet and as uncomplaining.   *Goes,* L.

Dr. S. Well, Herbert, my prescription, though a little unpalatable, has turned out efficacious after all.

Herb. Complete—our happiness is now assured.

Dr. S. Then, you'll have no objection to my presenting my little bill. (*gives challenge*)

Herb. My challenge—William, forgive me.

Dr. S. (*tears the paper*) Herbert, it is forgotten for ever.

Pinch. How delightful to the philanthropic mind it is to see the chords of human sympathy vibrate in harmonious unison : can I venture to hope that, however irregular some of my practices may have been, the share I have had in bringing about so desirable a result will not be over-looked.

Dr. S. You, certainly, are entitled to our consideration. I am under especial obligations to you for the additional *éclat* with which you have surrounded my humble position, and when you have done as much honor to your own name, as you have brought discredit upon mine, we may hope to meet again.

Pinch. Under those circumstances, my dear Doctor, I fear that I shall have to augment the distress of the present gloomy hour, by bidding you an everlasting farewell.

Exit, R. 1 E.

Dr. S. Now that all is settled comfortable and happily, let us go to dinner.

HERB.   No, not yet;
    Our labour's done, 'tis true, but don't forget
    Ere we can dine, the moral we must shew.
DR. S. Moral! they've seen that, bless you, long ago,
    Or else the Author's lost his time and pains,
    In any case one comfort still remains;
    They cannot blame us if we but aspire
    To please our Patrons and to PLAY WITH FIRE.

Curtain.

Printed by Thomas Scott, Warwick Court, Holborn.